DOWN ON FRIENDLY ACRES

Fiddlesticks and gumdrop bars! Welcome to "Down on Friendly Acres," a series based on the life of a real family — my family — the Friend family. My parents were farmers. They raised crops, livestock, and me, along with my two brothers and sister, on a farm rightly named **Friendly Acres**.

I was raised on that farm in the 1950s and 1960s. Times were very different. Just ask your grandparents. The words **mall**, **computer**, **cell phone**, and **video game** weren't even in the dictionary. That's because there weren't any malls, computers, cell phones, or video games.

I was born on April 6, 1955. In that year there were only forty-eight states, a stamp cost three pennies, a loaf of bread cost eighteen cents, and Barbie wasn't even "born" yet.

With two older brothers, Ronald and Duane, a younger sister, Diane, and lots of cousins, there was always some fussin' and fightin' going on. That's where Grandma Brombaugh came in. On April 9, 2006, Grandma Brombaugh turned ninety-nine years young. She was and still remains the "wise" one.

My dad and mom, Harold and Jean Friend, were always friendly, loving, and kind — even though life wasn't always friendly, loving, and kind to them. They both had very difficult childhoods.

My father, the youngest of eight children, recalls the heartache when his parents separated in the 1930s. Back then only a handful of marriages ended in divorce. As a fifth grader, my dad recalls clutching a tobacco corn knife in his hand as he helped load his belongings onto the neighbor's cattle truck to move to a new home. That knife soon represented how his family was torn apart and his heart ripped in two.

My mother, an only child, was in second grade when her father was accidentally electrocuted while working on a power line during a terrible thunderstorm. Mother cried herself to sleep, awaking the next morning to realize she would never be able to say goodbye to the father she had adored.

Heartbreaking moments — we all have them. For my father it was a home divided and for my mother a father gone without warning. But they both taught me it's what you do with those heartbreaking moments that counts. My parents met, fell in love, and were determined to provide a home where there was lots of love, joy, and peace.

You may be going through a heartbreaking moment in your life. You can choose to rise above your heartache and your pain. My parents did. And that's why I have written this series. As my Grandma Brombaugh would say, "They not only talked the talk, they walked the walk!"

So come on down on **Friendly Acres** *with me. "We will laugh - cry - shout with jubilation - sing - dance - join the celebration. We will love - share - feel the good vibrations - down on* **Friendly Acres** *with me!"*

Fiddlesticks and gumdrop bars. *I've run out of room! Remember,*

I'M A FRIEND
and U R 2!

R. Friend

DEDICATION

. . . in memory and honor of my mother, Jean Friend, who showed us all how to sow seeds of a different kind.
. . . with gratitude and love to my father, Harold Friend, who is still sowing those seeds.
. . . to my Grandma Brombaugh for all her wisdom, love, patience, and perseverance.
. . . and to my husband, Bill, and my children, Jeremy and Stephanie, for their endless love and encouragement.

R. FRIEND

Swallows Her Pride

Down On
Friendly Acres
#1

SUNFLOWER SEEDS PRESS

ISBN 0-9743627-0-0

Text copyright © 2003 "R. Friend" Ronda Friend
Illustrations by Bill Ross
Graphic design - Julie Wanca Design

All rights reserved. Published by Sunflower Seeds Press, PO Box 1476, Franklin, Tennessee 37065

Library of Congress Control Number 2003095592

Printed in the U.S.A.

First Printing, Second Printing, Third Printing, Fourth Printing, Fifth Printing, Sixth Printing.
Sunflower Seeds Press

CONTENTS

The Friend Family

Duane, Ronda, Diane, and Ronald

I'm A Friend!

Fiddlesticks and gumdrop bars. Somebody help! If you are readin' this book, which you must be, **I NEED HELP!** It's my name. It's drivin' me nuts and bananas. Let me explain. I'm a friend. You are too. But I really am a FRIEND.

Hear me out. I don't want to make a big deal about my name. But my name is Ronda Jean. You spell my first name R-o-n-d-a. Most Rhondas I know spell their name with an "h." That would make it R-h-o-n-d-a.

It doesn't take a tree full of owls to know that if you put an "h" in Ronda it wouldn't be Ronda. It would be Rrrr-honda. *Now, I don't have a Honda. And there's no "h" in Ronda.*

Like I said, I don't want to make a big deal about my name. BUT YOU SPELL MY NAME R-O-N-D-A.

I'm a farmer's daughter. And I'm pleased as a pig in mud to be one! *Hungh, hungh, hungh.* Excuse me. I snort when I get excited.

Oh, I almost forgot the most important part — my last name. I'm a Friend.

If I tell someone I've never met before my name, they say, "You're a what?"

And I say, "I'm a Friend."

And they say, "We just met. How do you know you're my friend?"

And I say, "No, no, no. I'm R. Friend."

And they say, "Our friend, your friend, my friend. I don't care! WHAT'S YOUR NAME?"

And I say, "My name is Ronda Jean Friend. R-o-n-d-a J-e-a-n F-r-i-e-n-d or R. Friend for short."

Then the stranger says, "Why didn't you say so in the first place? So you spell your name R-h-o-..."

And I interrupt them to say, "I don't want to make a big deal about my name. BUT YOU SPELL MY NAME R-O-N-D-A F-R-I-E-N-D. And I'm a farmer's daughter. I am pleased as a pig in mud to be one! *Hungh, hungh, hungh.*"

My daddy's name is Harold Eugene. My momma's name is Jean Vivian. Daddy is a joker. When he first saw my momma, he thought she was cute. He found out her name. Then he went up to her and said, "I'm Harold *EUGENE. YOU JEAN?* Would you like to be my *FRIEND?*"

My momma thought he was funny and cute. So cute she called him "eye candy." That's cuter than cute.

You can tell that my parents love each other bunches. Momma calls it being lovey-dovey. They are always holdin' hands, kissin', and givin' each other *goo-goo eyes*.

Goo-goo eyes are when you smile at someone with your eyeballs. You roll your eyes this way and that way. Then you blink and wink your eyes real fast like a humming-bird flappin' its wings.

My parents are one of the friendliest couples I know. And I'm not just saying that because our last name is Friend. But come to think of it, it would be very hard to be mean with a name like Friend.

People around these parts say the Friend family has never met a stranger they didn't know. That is 'cause we Friends love to talk 'n talk 'n talk.

Sooner or later we find out, if we talk to somebody long enough, that we know somebody, who knows somebody, who knows somebody, who knows them. So now the stranger is a friend too.

I reckon if I sat down with you, I would find out that I know somebody, who knows somebody, who knows somebody, who knows you. And even if we didn't, you could still be my friend. Why?

'Cause...
I'M A FRIEND
and U R 2!

CHAPTER 2

Down On Friendly Acres

We live on a farm just outside a little town called Dadsville. We moved there in 1959. My parents named our farm *Friendly Acres*.

My daddy works two jobs. During the day he works in a factory. He makes a lot of money — fifteen dollars a day — sixty dollars a week! And at night he works on our farm.

We love living on *Friendly Acres*. I wrote a song about our farm. My piano teacher, Mrs. Shipley, helped me put it down on paper. I can only play the melody right now. It goes like this:

Come On Down On Friendly Acres

by R. Friend

My momma loves everything about being a farmer's wife. Well, almost everything. The only thing she doesn't like about farm life is the smell.

On a hot, humid day, *Friendly Acres* stinks to high heaven. We have lots of cattle, pigs, sheep, chickens, and one horse. That makes for a lot of stinky you-know-what!

A couple days ago the air was horrible. It was so bad we wore bandanas around our noses and mouths. That was the day Momma wrote a poem about the smell.

There are baby bovine beauties,
plump piglets poised to scram,
a foal that frolics in the field
and lovely lit-
tle lambs.

They're cute, they're sweet
but take a whiff — the air it smells p.u.
No diapers or potty training here — it's one
big stinkaroo!

When the farm really starts to stink so bad that you can't breathe, Momma just plops a clothespin on her nose. She looks funny and it's hard to breathe, but she's a-smilin'.

Momma smiles a lot. She loves being a farmer's wife and the mother of four children. Growin' up she was an only child.

Momma missed having brothers and sisters. She would pretend to have siblings but not by playing with dolls. They cost too much money. She used bugs — big bugs, little bugs, live bugs, dead bugs. Bugs would be her guests as she sat down for tea and cookies. She loved being surrounded by bugs.

Momma's still surrounded by bugs today, of the human kind. There are four of us — Ronald, Duane, Ronda, and Diane.

18

When it comes to being buggy, Daddy says, "My kids are the pests — I mean best!"

I told you he's a joker.

Ronald is the oldest Friend. My parents say, "Ronald, you should know better, you're the oldest."

He doesn't know any better. How could he? He's the firstborn. He doesn't have anybody to watch to know any better. And besides, where do they think he got so smart?

Next there's Duane. In some ways we are as different as night and day. But Duane and I do have several things in common. We like to talk 'n talk 'n talk and fuss 'n fuss 'n fight! Momma says every day we get better and better at fussin' 'n fightin'.

Then there's me, remember, R-O-N-D-A without an "h." Momma named me that way 'cause she wanted it to be special — different. Dad thinks I'm special. Duane thinks I'm different.

Last there's Diane. She's the baby. She never gets in trouble. That's 'cause everybody thinks she's an angel. Everybody doesn't live with her. I do. Who are they kidding? She's not an angel. She's a *"hawkephant."*

Hold on to your pants. Let me explain. There's a big hawk in our woods. She built a huge nest at the top of a pine tree. Daddy told me that most animals see in black and white, but hawks can see in color. They have a great pair of eyes — big eyes like my sister.

And then there are elephants. Ronald learned at school that elephants have great memories. I guess that's why their ears are so huge.

What does that have to do with my baby sister? Well, Diane is always watchin' us like a hawk. Then she remembers like an elephant what we did to get in trouble. She knows what NOT to do. That's why I call her a "hawkephant!" Or I guess you could say she's a "hawkephant" TRYING to be an angel.

If there's an angel in our family, it's not my sister. It's my grandma — Grandma Brombaugh. She can't fly. She doesn't have wings or a halo. Although, she's always wearing hats. I don't *think* she has a halo.

Oh well, don't let her looks fool you. Momma says, "Grandma Brombaugh has more wisdom in her little pinky than some people do in their whole bodies."

My grandma, Edna Viola Peters Brombaugh, was born in 1907. I know for a fact she is an undercover angel. Angels always wear white dresses.

When Grandma was ten, she tried on a pair of pants and couldn't stand them. She has never worn anything to this day except a dress.

Grandma's always asking me if her slip is showing. And her slip just happens to be white. Therefore I have come to the conclusion that the so-called "slip" is just her angel costume peeking out from under her dress. She is an undercover angel.

And Grandma Brombaugh wants to turn everyone she meets into an angel too. Daddy says she's got her work cut out for her down on *Friendly Acres.*

CHAPTER 3

Daddy's Not Just A Farmer

At the back of *Friendly Acres* are some big woods. In the middle of our farm we have a little creek. And up on the hill we have a pond. That's where I love to go fishin'.

The best part of fishin' is putting the worm on the hook. Here's what you do. Pick out a worm. Make sure it's big and fat. A short, stubby one works best.

Find the end and then the middle. That's what I call the "enddle." The "enddle" — middle of the end — is where you put the hook. Try not to squirm, on account of whatever was on the inside of that worm is now on the outside of the worm. You know you hit the "enddle" when that brown goop starts drippin' down your fingers. It smells — p.u.!

You'll want to hold your nose. But don't, on account of that brown mushy stuff. It will start drippin' down your nose. People will think your nose is runnin'. That's not a good thing.

Now, where was I? Oh yeah, back to the worm. That little worm is not going to like it one bit. He'll try as hard as he can to wiggle himself out of your hands. But just like God made macaroni for cheese, bugs for birds, and peanut butter for jelly, He made worms for fish.

The hardest part about fishin' is when the fish eats more than the worm. My grandma says, "That fish ate the whole kit and caboodle."

Most of the time, you can work that hook right off. But sometimes it can be down-right stubborn. 'Specially if the fish eats what Dad calls hook, line, and sinker. That's when you need special pliers.

Don't tell anybody. I got these from my dad's tackle box. I'm not suppose to get in my dad's tackle box without his say so. But I reckon he won't mind me showing you his special pliers.

These "hook-out" pliers can get way down in a fish's mouth — all the way to its little tummy. It just takes experience. Before you can say, *"fiddlesticks and gumdrop bars,"* out comes the hook, line, and sinker.

My Grandmother Brombaugh says, "Experience is the best teacher." If that's true, I reckon experience is what makes my daddy the best teacher I know.

Daddy was born in 1922, the baby of eight children. Growing up on the farm, his favorite project was making things grow. My daddy remembers playing in his sandbox. He would sit tops of pineapples or stems of roses in the sand, then water them and watch them grow.

My daddy's not just a farmer!

My daddy's a weatherman. He can tell by the way the leaves are blowing on the old oak tree if it's going to rain or not.

My daddy's not just a farmer!

My daddy's a veterinarian — an animal doctor. He knows when a cow has a tummyache. That's when he mixes up what he calls a "concoction." He heats up some lard or grease and mixes it with turpentine. He puts it in an old Coke bottle. Then he "drenches the bloated cow." That's farm talk for makin' a cow with a fat tummy open her mouth and take her medicine. In a few minutes she's good to go.

My daddy's not just a farmer!

My daddy's a great fisherman. He can tell the day before if it will be good fishin' or not. If the sky is red at night, it's sailors' delight. But if it's red in the morning, it's sailors' warnin'. He even knows what rocks most of the worms are hidin' under.

Daddy says that fishin' is not only good for the body, it's good for the soul.

I love it when I catch lots of fish. We have a big fish fry. But on the other hand, I don't mind when I don't catch a thing. That gives me lots of time for daydreamin'.

There's nothing better than daydreamin' — except *fiddlesticks and gumdrop bars*. But that's another story.

CHAPTER 4

I'm Not A Spoiled Brat!

I love everything about life down on *Friendly Acres*. I love milkin' the cows. I love Charley, my Polled Hereford calf. I love wadin' barefoot in the creek and catching tadpoles. I really, really love playin' hide and seek with my cousins in the woods. I don't even mind sloppin' the hogs.

Oops! I bet you don't even know what sloppin' the hogs is all about. According to Noah - oh, not the guy who built the ark — although come to think about it, he had two hogs to slop. I mean Noah Webster.

Mr. Webster is the guy who wrote the book — *Noah Webster's Dictionary*. That book must weigh at least one hundred pounds.

It is the biggest book I've ever seen. Grandma says, "That book has more words than some-one could ever say in a lifetime."

Then she looks at me and smiles from ear to ear. She pats me on the head and says, "If anyone could say all those words in a life-time, it would be you."

"Thanks, Grandma. I think?"

Now, where was I? Oh yeah, back to Noah. Mr. Webster says that *slop,* s-l-o-p, is swill, s-w-i-l-l. Or swill is slop. Either way slop . . .

---

[1]slop / **'släp** / *noun* / 4 a : food waste (as garbage) fed to animals : <u>SWILL</u>

. . . or swill is "garbage or waste mixed with water." *Fiddlesticks and gumdrop bars!* No wonder pigs stink. P.U. ! ! !

I don't care. I still like sloppin' the hogs. Except for the time I did it with my brother, Duane. It all started the night of my birthday.

On my sixth birthday, April 6, 1961, I didn't get everything I wanted. I wanted a scooter and a new outfit for my Chatty Cathy doll.

Every girl I know wants a Chatty Cathy doll. And I have one. Chatty Cathy chats 'n chats 'n chats 'n chats. She'll talk your head off if you pull the string attached to the back of her neck.

My daddy says that Chatty Cathy reminds him of me. That is 'cause she loves to talk 'n talk 'n talk. He says there's only one difference. I can talk 'n talk 'n talk 'n you don't even have to pull my string. *(I don't have one.)*

I wanted a rolled up, long piece of black plastic. A rolled up piece of black plastic is more fun than a barrel of monkeys. Everyone has one, except me.

You roll it out flat on a hill. Then spray it down with a garden hose. After that you can slide-n-slip or slip-n-slide all you want. I just call it a slide-n-slip. I wanted one real bad, 'cause almost everybody I know has a slide-n-slip — except me.

I just wanted three things — a scooter, a new Chatty Cathy outfit, and a slide-n-slip. But what I wanted and what I got were two different things. Oh, I got my red, shiny scooter, and I liked it a lot. I rode it around our circle drive about fifty times.

But I didn't get a new outfit for my Chatty Cathy. Instead, I got a new tiny outfit for a little doll I got last Christmas. She's really tiny.

33

The doll's name is Bonnie. No, it's Betty. Oh no, it's Barbara — Barbie for short. Anyway, I don't play with her much. She's new, but who wants a Barbie doll? *Not me!*

And when I didn't get a slide-n-slip either, I was sad. I really wanted a slide-n-slip 'cause almost everybody I know has a slide-n-slip. My brother said I was poutin'. I wasn't poutin'!

I grabbed the dictionary and gave it to Grandma. She told me that according to *Noah Webster's Dictionary poutin'* is . . .

[1]pout / **ˈpaut** / *verb* / 1 a : to show displeasure by thrusting out the lips or wearing a sullen expression b : SULK.

. . . or in other words, my grandma said it's when your bottom lip looks like you got stung by a giant bumblebee.

I ran to the bathroom. I looked in the mirror. My lower lip was sort of big and poppin' out of my mouth. Ok, I guess you could say I pouted — but just a little.

Duane told me I got way too much for my birthday. And he said I should stop the poutin'. But he didn't stop there. Then he called me a name — a bad name — *a really bad name.* He pointed his finger at me and shouted, "Ronda, you are a *spoiled brat!*"

I didn't like the sound of those words — *spoiled* or *brat.* I surely didn't like them put together to describe me. Then I remembered. My Grandma Brombaugh always says, "If you don't have anything good to say about somebody — just don't say anything at all."

So I decided right then and there not to say another word all night. My lips were sealed. My mouth was shut.

CHAPTER 5

Clothespins

Do you know how hard it is to keep my mouth shut? You don't have to answer that. Well, after my party my head was about to burst on account of all those not-so-nice words I wanted to say to my brother. All kinds of ugly words were jumpin' 'round in my head like monkeys on a bed. They were trying to escape. I thought my head was going to pop off ! ! !

I'm not a *spoiled brat!* I'll see what Noah has to say. Grandma helped me look up those words in *Noah Webster's Dictionary*.

---

²spoiled / **'spoi(&)ld** / *verb* / 3 a : to damage seriously : RUIN / b : to impair the quality or effect of / 4 a : to impair the disposition or character of by overindulgence or excessive praise.

---

brat / **'brat** / *noun* / 1 a: <u>CHILD</u>; specifically : an ill-mannered annoying child.

Grandma Brombaugh says that *spoiled* means "to demand or expect too much." And *brat* means "hard to keep under control."

I don't demand or expect too much! I'm just a tad upset that I don't get everything I want. And I'm not hard to control. I know how to control myself. I'll show my brother. My lips are sealed and my mouth is shut.

I kept my mouth closed for nine hours. Zzzzzzzzzzzzzzz *(loud snoring)*. Ok, it was while I was sleepin'. When I woke up, it was rainin' cats and dogs.

Daddy told my brother and me to go slop the hogs. I thought, "If the rain keeps up those pigs can slop themselves."

My brother Duane and I put on our yellow slickers and boots and headed to the pig shed. Only one problem, my head was still pounding. Those not-so-nice words I wanted to call my brother were like Mexican jumpin' beans bouncing off the walls of my brain. I thought they were going to pop out any minute!

I didn't want to be a brat, you know, hard to control. I needed to keep my words inside my head. So I used clothespins. I decided to close off any way those words could get out of my head.

I put a clothespin on my nose. Those words could escape through my nostrils. I put clothespins on my ears, on account of those not so-nice-words could sneak out of my ears. My brother looked at me and said, "What do you think you're doin'?"

I said, "My head is spinning with words I want to call you. But I'm not going to say one word. They are not coming out of this head. I am closing off all the ways they could escape from my head. My nose, my ears . . ."

And then I placed a BIG clothespin on my mouth. And I said, "**mbmlblbmm!!!!!**"

After about fifteen seconds I took the clothespin off my mouth, on account of the fact that I COULDN'T BREATHE!

I told Duane that I didn't appreciate him calling me a *spoiled brat*. I was a little upset 'cause I didn't get a slide-n-slip for my birthday. I couldn't help it. Without warnin', my bottom lip swelled up and stuck out.

I said, "Duane, you hurt my feelings. And besides, almost everybody I know has a slide-n-slip."

And my brother said, "There you go again. You're pouting. You good-for-nothin' *spoiled brat!*"

The clothespins were coming off. Before I could help it, a couple of not-so-nice words just plopped right out of my mouth.

I yelled, "I'd rather be a spoiled brat then a **big, fat rat like you!**"

He said, "Oh, yeah!"
"**Oh yeah!**"
"OH, YEAH!"
"OH, YEAH, YEAH!"

Four "brats" and three "rats" later we tackled each other. Yuck! We ended up in the pig pen — mud, slop, and you-know-what!

I was knee deep in all that yucky muck. The more we wrestled, the more Duane and I realized that we were having way too much fun to be fightin'. A miracle happened! We stopped our fussin' 'n fightin'.

Partly because we didn't want to get any of that mud, slop, or you-know-what in our mouths, and partly because we were having more fun than a barrel of monkeys. Or maybe I should say a pen of pigs.

I am a farmer's daughter. And now I know just how pleased a pig in mud can be. Hungh, hungh, hungh.

I didn't get a slide-n-slip for my birthday. But rolling around in all that mud was way more fun than that old piece of black plastic could ever be.

CHAPTER 6

Swallowing My Pride

We were having a hay day when something terrible happened! Out of the blue, a loud voice shouted — **"DUANE HAMILTON FRIEND!"**

"RONDA JEAN FRIEND!"

It's bad news when your parents use your middle name. But when they use your last name too — that spells one big word.

T-R-O-U-B-L-E. **TROUBLE!** T-R-O-U-B-L-E! *And we were in it!*

Momma said, "RONDA JEAN! Get out of that pig pen right this instant."

Daddy hosed us down to clean us up. Momma dried us off and set us down. Before you could say, *"fiddlesticks and gumdrop bars,"* we were in our own little corners.

42

Momma looked at me and said, "DON'T YOU MOVE!"

I don't know why mommies and daddies say, "DON'T YOU MOVE!" Because when they say "DON'T YOU MOVE," it makes you want to move even more. But I didn't! I stayed put!

Out of the corner of my eye I saw my baby sister - "Miss Hawkephant." She doesn't know how to write or spell. But I could tell she was taking notes in her head on how NOT to be like me. I can't remember the last time Diane was in time-out. And there I was in my time-out corner again.

Now don't get me wrong. Time-out isn't the greatest. But my Grandma Brombaugh always says, "When life gives you lemons, make lemonade."

So I thought, "If Cinderella liked her corner, why can't I like mine?"

You remember Cinderella? Or as her mean sisters would say, "**Cinddderrrellllaaa!**"

Cinderella loved her corner so much she sang a song about it! So I thought and I thought, and I came up with my own little song for my own teeny, tiny corner. It goes like this. . .

In my teeny, tiny corner,
in my teeny, tiny chair,
I can dream of what I want to be!
Close my eyes — make believe
and I can be anywhere.
Just watch me poof! One-Two-Three.

I'm a martial artist and
my kick just hit my brother.
I'm a doctor sewing up his nose.
I'm a fisherman who's caught
a great blue marlin.
I'm a ballerina striking a sweet pose.

In my teeny, tiny corner,
in my teeny, tiny chair,
I can dream of what I want to be.

Oh no! Did you hear that? Shh!!!
I have bad news. And I have badder news.

The *bad news* is time is up for time-out! I have to get out of my corner.

The *badder news* is that I have to go make it right with my brother. I'd rather give him a right, and then a left, and then another right.

I ran to Grandma Brombaugh and cried, "I *hafta* 'pologize."

She replied, "Ronda, that is the best thing you can ever do."

"That's easy for you to say — you're not the one 'pologizing. And don't forget, he called me a bad name first."

"Ronda Jean! First, last, it doesn't matter. Part of growing up is learning to apologize. Most of the time we just have to swallow our pride."

"Swallow our pride? Grandma, what's that all about?"

Without even asking Noah, Grandma answered, "Pride is sometimes thinking that you are better than anyone else, including your brother. Imagine those not-so-nice words that were stuck in your head are stuck in your throat."

She handed me a cookie and a glass of milk. "Pretend the cookie is the not-so-nice words and chew them all up. Then take a drink of milk and swallow. Poof! Those not-so-nice words will disappear and you will feel all clean inside."

Well, I did it! I swallowed the cookie and my pride. I 'pologized to Duane. It made me feel lots better — inside and out. Grandma was right. I felt good all over.

I felt like, like, like an angel . . .

OH, NO!!! I ran to the bathroom to look in the mirror. You know Grandma. She's an angel and wants to turn everyone she meets into an angel too.

Thank heaven! No halo, no wings!

Whew! I can't be an angel and keep up the fussin' 'n fightin' with my brother, too. And besides, I don't have a white slip.

CHAPTER 7

"Turkey Lips!"

Before supper I went outside to play with my dogs, Teeny and Tiny. *Fiddlesticks and gumdrop bars!* I heard a huge commotion!

My brother was yelling at the top of his lungs. **"I've got a turkey caught in my throat!"**

"I've got a turkey caught in my throat!"

I ran to the kitchen. There was Duane with his mouth open like a large mouth bass. I hollered, "You have a *whole turkey* caught in your throat?"

He shouted, "No, you *turkey lips!* I have a piece of turkey caught in my throat. See!" Duane opened his mouth and said, "Aaaahhhhh!"

I couldn't believe it! There was a piece of turkey. I replied, "You better watch what you say! You're going to have to swallow your *pride* and your *turkey* too."

Duane had snuck a piece of turkey — crust and all — out of the oven before supper. He was still able to breathe and swallow. He just couldn't swallow the turkey. The piece of turkey was curled up and stuck in his throat.

I didn't want him to choke. Besides, I wouldn't have anybody to fuss 'n fight with if somethin' ever happened to him. So I remembered that when my baby sister, Diane, gets something caught in her throat, Momma turns her upside down, and then pats her on the back.

I went to pick Duane up and turn him upside down. Duane said, "What are you doing?"

"I'm trying to turn you upside down, but you're too big!"

Duane said, "I know, I'll stand on my head. Then I'll be upside down."

I smiled real big. Then I lifted my hand in the air and chuckled, "This is going to hurt me more than it hurts you!"

I started patting him on the back over and over and over . . .

"Stop, Ronda. Stop!"

I turned my head upside down and said, "Say 'aaahhh.'"

Duane did. And the turkey was still there. It was just sitting there between his tonsils and that little flapper thing.

That turkey wouldn't go down. And it wouldn't come up.

I said, "I know the problem. You shouldn't have called me *'turkey lips'*. Now's the time to swallow your *pride* and your *turkey* too."

I gave him a piece of bread and a glass of water. (Cookies and milk would have spoiled his supper.) He swallowed once. He opened his mouth and said, "Aaahhh."

The turkey was still there.

I gave him another piece of bread and some more water. Duane opened his mouth and said, "Aaahhh."

The turkey was still there.

It looked as if he wasn't going to be able to swallow his pride on his own after all. That turkey was "stuck like a wet pig."

I had an idea! "I'll be right back!"

I came right back with these special fishin' pliers from Dad's tackle box.

Duane said, "You got into Dad's tackle box!"

"This is an **EMERGENCY!** Oh, and don't worry. I ran some hot water over them. It took the worm crud right off. Duane, just open your mouth and say 'aaahhh!'"

And just when I started to fix the problem, I heard someone yellin'.

"RONDA JEAN!!!"

"Fiddlesticks and gumdrop bars! Here we go again."

My parents walked in the kitchen. "What in heaven's name are you doing?"

I replied, "I was just trying to help. Duane can't seem to swallow his pride . . . I mean his turkey."

And they said, "What? A turkey!"

We explained everything. Momma and Daddy told us they appreciated us working together to solve the problem.

Daddy reminded me that I was *never* to get into his fishin' tackle box without his permission.

Momma told me to *never ever* put something down my throat or my brother's throat ever again. And when there is an emergency, we need to come find them.

We both felt awful. Just then, out of the corner of my eye, I spied "Miss Hawkephant" spyin' on my brother and me. There she was again — *taking notes in her head.*

If I keep teaching Diane what not to do, she WILL grow up to be an angel. And it will be all my fault! I will have created an angel! *Fiddlesticks and gumdrop bars!*

Now, where was I? Oh, yeah! Back to 'pologizing! As much as I hate to admit it, it does make me feel better inside and out.

CHAPTER 8

Rotten Eggs

We still had a problem. The turkey was still stuck in Duane's throat.

No matter what my brother did, the turkey wouldn't come out!!!

My momma studied to be a nurse. She said, "We are going to have to keep an eye on Duane."

I mumbled, "No problem! I'll just get *'Miss Hawkephant.'*"

Momma asked, "What did you say?"

I said, "No problem! I'll get some *chalk 'n hunt* for paper. Then Duane and I can play together."

Momma said, "How nice, Ronda. That's sweet, but Duane can help me."

Duane was getting a lot of attention — too much if you ask me. Momma and Grandma had him helpin' in the kitchen. I was in the front room *pretendin'* I wasn't listening.

Grandma Brombaugh baked all the home-made bread, rolls, and desserts in the school cafeteria when my momma and daddy went to school. She was making my favorite — peanut butter fudge. Grandma couldn't go anywhere without people asking for her peanut butter fudge.

And Duane was readin' the recipe. . .

PEANUT BUTTER FUDGE

In a saucepan mix 2 cups sugar
and 2/3 cup milk.
Cook until soft boiled
and add 1 cup peanut butter
and 1 cup marshmallow fluff.
Pour into an eight by eight inch
buttered dish immediately.
Let cool. Slice and serve.

Grandma said, "Duane, you are such a good reader. That was so sweet of you."

Duane said, "No, Grandma Brombaugh. You're the one that's sweet. In fact, you're much sweeter than your peanut butter fudge."

Yuck! My brother was butterin' up my grandma. And she loved every minute of it. Besides, he was gettin' to sample everything. Duane licked the peanut butter fudge spoon clean.

Grandma was also making her famous homemade rolls. As Tony the Tiger would say, *"They're Grrrrrrreeeeaaaatttt!"*

That's because of the secret ingredient. I'd tell you what it is, but then it wouldn't be a secret anymore.

Duane popped his head into the front room and asked, "Ronda, would you like to help us make DEVILED eggs?"

He whispered, "You'd be good at that!"

I stuck my tongue out and said, "Sure! I like peelin' the shells off the eggs."

(Really I just wanted an excuse to get some free samples.)

Momma was cutting the eggs in half when she cried, "P.U."! ! !

"What's wrong, Momma?"

"This egg is *spoiled*. It's *spoiled rotten* to the core!"

She held the egg up to my nose and I hollered, "Gross — that's disgustin'!"

Duane mumbled, *"Sis, you stink!"*

Momma asked, "Duane, what did you say?"

"This egg reeks!"

I whispered, "Fast thinking!"

61

We were fannin' our noses trying to breathe some fresh air. Meanwhile Momma smiled and handed us each some clothespins. We wrapped up the rotten egg and threw it in the garbage. Soon the air was clear. Dinner was served.

We all sat down for turkey, mashed potatoes, corn on the cob, deviled eggs, home-made rolls, and for dessert — peanut butter fudge.

I said the grace that evening. "…Thanks for only one spoiled rotten egg in the bunch and please don't let anyone else get turkey stuck in their throat. Amen."

And nobody else did.

Duane must have swallowed one hundred and sixty-seven times. *But the turkey was still there.*

CHAPTER 9

Haftas

Supper was over and that meant only one thing. I had to do my *haftas*.

HAFTAS! HAFTAS! HAFTAS!

My parents make us do our *haftas* everyday. That evening I had Grandma Brombaugh look up *haftas* to see what Webster had to say. Grandma said *hafta* wasn't in Noah's book.

So I told Momma, "Accordin' to Grandma, '*hafta*' isn't a word."

And guess what?

Momma said, "*Hafta* is a word. *Hafta* is a good word. And *haftas* are good for us."

And then I said, "*Hafta, h-a-f-t-a,* isn't a word! It isn't even in the dictionary!"

And guess what?

Momma said, "*Hafta* is a made up word and short for you 'have to,' which means *do what you're told because Daddy or I say so.*"

She ended with saying that *hafta* was in HER dictionary.

I wanted to say, "I didn't know you had a dictionary."

Instead, I swallowed. *(gulp)*

Momma said, "What are you doing?"

I said, "I'm swallowin'."

"Swallowing what?" she asked.

"You know. I'm swallowin' my pride."

She smiled and gave me a big hug.

After my *haftas*, Momma and I sat down and wrote a poem together. Instead of reading me a story before bedtime, Momma read Chatty Cathy and me our poem.

HAFTA, HAFTA, HAFTA

I *hafta* rise and shine and be at school by eight.
I *hafta* do my homework and not stay up too late!
I *hafta* raise my hand and not chew gum at all.
I *hafta* say "yes ma'am" and never spit spitballs.

I *hafta* get in line. I *hafta* wait my turn.
I *hafta* take a nap. I *hafta* live and learn.
I *hafta*, *hafta*, *hafta*. I *hafta* day and night.
When I *hafta*, *hafta*, *hafta* — it makes me so uptight.

I *hafta* sit up straight and not act like a clown.
I *hafta* hurry up. I *hafta* slow it down.
I *hafta* take a bath. I *hafta* comb my hair.
I *hafta* brush my teeth — put on clean underwear.

I *hafta* drink my milk. I *hafta* eat my peas.
I *hafta* use my manners, say things like pretty please.
I *hafta* clean my room and put my toys away.
It's all a part of growing up and learning to obey.

You think with all the haftas — they'd make me go berserk!
Momma says that haftas are laying the groundwork!
'Cause someday soon I'll grow up and my haftas I'll outgrow.
My hafta list will change and begin to overflow!

I'll have to rise and shine and be at work by six.
I'll have to mow the lawn and pick up all the sticks.
I'll have to walk the dog and fix those things he chews.
I'll have to clean up accidents like p.u. — doggie doos.

I'll have to doctor scratches and wipe those snotty noses.
I'll have to mop up throw up —
then make things smell like roses.
I'll have to nurse kids back to health
and stay up most the night.
I'll have to interfere and break up all those fights.

Doing all these haftas now is just my way of showing —
How much I love my parents. Hey! I can wait on growing.
When asked to do my haftas — there's no need to blow up!
After all is said and done —
I don't really want to grow up!!!

When she finished, I gave her a kiss and a hug and a love around the neck. And then I said, "I'm sorry."

She said, "For what?"

I said, "For being a *poutin', spoiled brat* on my birthday just 'cause I didn't get everything I wanted."

She smiled and gave me a kiss and a hug and a love around the neck.

Momma said, "Honey, I know you were a little disappointed on your birthday. Daddy and I would give you the moon if we could."

I thought, "*I didn't want the moon*, I just wanted a rolled up piece of black plastic."

Momma continued, "I made your new doll, Barbie, some clothes out of scraps of material to save money. Even though Daddy works in town, we have to watch our pennies."

Then she handed that tiny doll to me and said, "And I was hoping that you would start playing with your Barbie doll a little. She might feel left out. Besides, someday she might be very popular."

I whispered, "That will *never* happen!"

Momma added, "Oh, and I almost forgot. We had enough money left to get you a roll of black plastic, but the hardware store was out. I guess everybody has a slide-n-slip. They've ordered more, and it will be in next week."

"Oh, no! Momma, *I don't want it!*"

Momma asked, "What's wrong darling, are you not feeling well?"

"I'm feeling fine. I just don't want to smell bad!"

"Smell bad?"

"Yeah, I don't want to be *spoiled* — you know, like a *rotten egg!*"

I gave her a big kiss, a big hug, and a big love around the neck. She gave me a bigger kiss, a bigger hug, and a bigger love around the neck.

Then I pulled her string — Chatty Cathy's string that is. Momma doesn't have one. I pulled Chatty Cathy's string until she said my favorite phrase over and over again.

"I love you! I love you! I love you!"

THE END

P.S. The next mornin' I woke up and ran into my brother's room hollering, "Wake up! Wake up, Duane! Say 'aaahhh!'"

He opened his mouth like a wide mouth bass and you won't believe it!!! *The turkey was . . .*

To *find out what happens you'll have to*
read the next book!

Keep your eyes peeled
and look for the sunflowers!
Every full illustration in this book
has a sunflower hidden in the page.

Happy hunting!

Daddy
Harold Eugene

Momma
Jean Vivian

Duane, Ronda, Diane, and Ronald

Friendly Acres Farm

My parent's
Wedding

Grandma & Grandpa
Brombaugh

Grandma Brombaugh's
Peanut Butter Fudge

In a saucepan mix 2 cups sugar
and 2/3 cup milk.
Cook until soft boiled
and add 1 cup peanut butter
and 1 cup marshmallow fluff.
Pour into an eight by eight inch
buttered dish immediately.
Let cool. Slice and serve.

Grandma
Brombaugh

As Grandma Brombaugh would say, *"The cat's out of the bag!"* What's Grandma Brombaugh's secret ingredient in her homemade rolls? It's mashed potatoes! Here's her famous recipe. There's no telling how many potato rolls my grandmother has made for family, friends, and **Friends**.

Grandma Brombaugh's Homemade Potato Yeast Rolls

1 pkg. dried yeast

1 cup warm water (105 -115 degrees - can be water that potatoes were cooked in)

2/3 C. sugar

1 t. salt

2/3 C shortening (oleo or oil)

2 eggs

1 C. mashed potatoes - still lukewarm

7 - 71/2 C. all purpose white flour

Directions:

Dissolve yeast in warm water in a very large mixing bowl. Stir in the sugar and salt. Then add shortening and eggs. Mix in the potatoes and 4 cups of flour. Beat until smooth. Mix in enough remaining flour to make dough easy to handle. Turn the dough onto a lightly floured surface. Knead until smooth and elastic. (Takes about five minutes.) Place in another very large greased bowl. (The dough will rise even in the refrigerator so it is important to put in a big bowl so that the cover won't "blow off" because of the dough doubling in size. If you are going to be baking the rolls the same day use a wet tea towel to cover the bowl.) Cover tightly and refrigerate at least eight hours and no longer than five days before baking.

My second favorite part in making Grandma Brombaugh's refrigerated rolls is coming up! Punch dough down with fist. Of course, make sure you've washed your hands. Shape the dough into doughnut hole size balls. Place three in each section of a greased muffin pan and let rise until double in size. Bake at 350 degrees until lightly brown. Depending on oven this will take 8-10 minutes.

My favorite part is **EATING** Grandma Brombaugh's rolls — hot with butter and homemade strawberry jelly!

There's No End In Friend

by R. Friend

Check Our Our Websites

www.DownOnFriendlyAcres.com

What's fact and what's fiction in the "Down on Friendly Acres" series? Check out the website! There's art and writing contests, pictures, music, stories and more!

www.SunflowerSeedsPress.com

Check this website to see future book releases, book R. Friend for an author visit, enter the "Friend of R. Friend" author's contest, purchase cds, and much more!

"R. Friend - Time Out At Home"

This second book in the series is available for purchase on the websites. Here is a sneak preview!

Ronda's in trouble again. Duane's *still* in turkey trouble. And Ronda is afraid he's turning into one - beard, snood and wattle! Ronda's intentional trouble comes after hitting what would have been the winning home run until Duane tags her *out at home*. Ronda returns the favor by swinging her bat getting Duane *out at home*. Out of patience, Ronda finds herself in *time out at home* again! She takes to heart Grandma's advice, "Patience is the best remedy for any trouble!"

Order your copy today!

About the Author

Photo: Bob Fitzpenn

Ronda Friend (R. Friend) is a child at heart who has worked with children for over thirty years. As a storyteller, she has captivated hundreds of thousands of children with her music, animation, and big heart. She has directed and produced over twenty children's musicals. Ronda is the founder of Sunflower Seeds Press. As author of the *"Down on Friendly Acres"* series, her vision is to plant seeds of a different kind — seeds of kindness, patience, perseverance, laughter, and honesty into the lives of children.

She holds a B.A. degree in education with a minor in music. Ronda has two grown children, Jeremy and Stephanie, and lives with her husband, Bill, in Franklin, Tennessee.

Remember . . .
Grandma Brombaugh says,

"If you don't have anything good to say about somebody — just don't say anything at all."